OOGO THE CAVEBOY

By Christy Davis

STORY 1

Oogo was a small cave boy. He was seven summers old. He had long tangled dark brown hair and hazel green eyes. He wore a tiger skin and walked barefoot everywhere he went.

Oogo lived with his father and mother in a large cave up on the side of a big mountain. Four other people lived in the cave with them. Oogo was the only child.   Everyone helped find food and fight the big animals that came to eat them. They never let Oogo help, everyone thought that Oogo was too young.

Oogo loved to sit on the ledge in front of his cave when the dark clouds were up in the sky. He liked the feel of wind and rain on his face. He also liked to watch for lightning.

Christy Davis

3

When the lightning struck the earth, it would start a fire. Oogo's father and the other men would run down the mountain and bring some of the fire back to the cave. Everyone enjoyed its warmth.

One morning Oogo's father sat outside on the ledge in front of their cave. He had two stones, one in each

hand. He used one stone to sharpen the other. He was

chipping away pieces here and there, until at last he'd made a spearhead.

Oogo grabbed two rocks of his own. He beat them together as hard as he could. Oogo made so much noise his father turned around. He grabbed the stones from the boy's hands and tossed them away. "Ughh!" his father grunted.

Oogo picked up two more stones and snuck back inside the cave. Again he tried as hard as he could to chip out a spearhead like his father. "Ughh!" his mother grunted. She grabbed the stones and threw them to the ground.

Oogo sat quietly for a few minutes, but he grew tired of sitting. He knew his father and mother would be proud of him if he could make a spearhead. He picked up his two stones and went back outside.

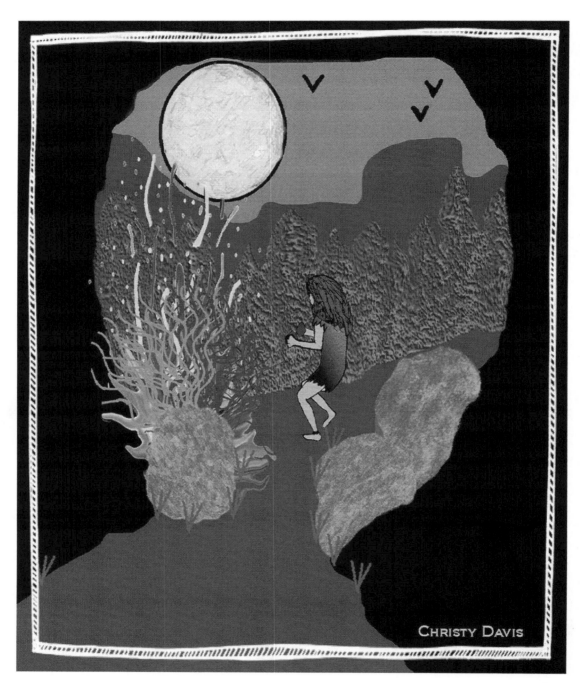

CHRISTY DAVIS

6

This time Oogo hid in a small patch of tall dry weeds near the cave and tried again. He beat the rocks together even harder this time. A spark flew from the rocks, and landed in a bush next to him. A small flame flickered up, and the brush caught fire.

Oogo jumped out of the brush and shouted for his father.

Everyone ran over to see what was wrong. They watched as the bush burn to the ground. Then, they looked up into the sky for the dark clouds and lightning. But the sky was bright blue. There were no clouds.

Ughh?" Oogo's father grunted. He wanted to know how the fire started.

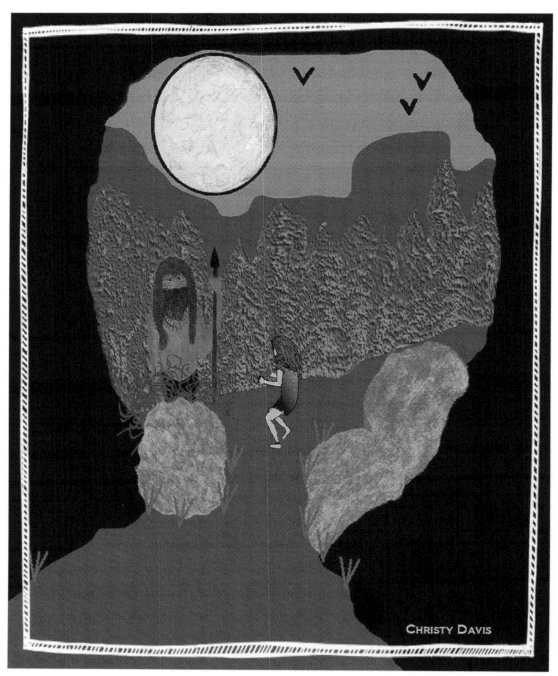

Oogo held out the two rocks and banged them together.

"Ughh?!" his father started to laugh. He didn't believe banging two rocks together could start a fire and neither did the others.

Oogo quickly gathered some dry weeds. He banged the stones together over and over, as fast, and as hard as he could. Poof! The dry weeds caught fire. Everyone stepped back. They were amazed. Oogo was a genius!

Oogo handed the stones to his father. His mother and father had already taught him that fire was dangerous. Oogo didn't like fire unless it was inside the cave where his father and the other men put it.

His father and mother hugged Oogo. They were very proud of their son. Now they could have fire to keep them warm whenever they wanted.

CHRISTY DAVIS

STORY 2

Oogo was a small cave boy. He was seven summers old. He had long tangled dark brown hair and hazel green eyes. He wore a tiger skin and walked barefoot everywhere he went.

Oogo lived with his father and mother in a large cave up on the side of a big mountain. Four other people lived in the cave with them. Oogo was the only child. Everyone helped find food and fight the big animals that came to eat them. They never let Oogo help, everyone thought that Oogo was too young.

One warm summer morning Oogo and his parents followed the others down the mountain. They were going to find food. Wild nuts and berries grew along the banks of a stream not far away.

CHRISTY DAVIS

14

Oogo loved to go to the stream. He liked to eat berries and nuts. He also liked to swim. He'd been swimming for two summers now. He was always careful to stay near the shore. He always made sure the water never went over his head, and he never went swimming alone.

After everyone picked the nuts and berries, the men speared fish in the river. No one ever let him spear fish, but Oogo didn't mind. Instead he played in the water next to his mother.

Soon it began to get dark. Everyone gathered all the nuts, berries, and fish, and walked back to their cave to divide the food.

Oogo's mother handed him a piece of raw fish to eat, but Oogo didn't want it. He hated fish. He couldn't even stand the smell of it.

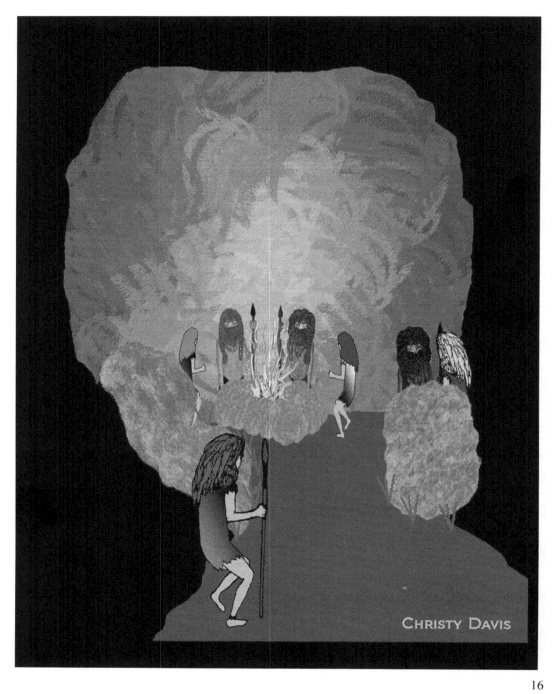

CHRISTY DAVIS

16

Oogo sat quietly for a while, trying to think of a good place to hide it. Somewhere his parents would never find it. Finally Oogo decided to burn it. He stuck the chunk of fish on a long stick and hung it out over the fire.

Oogo thought he'd solved his problem without anyone noticing, until everyone around him began sniffing the air and grunting. And when he looked up he saw the others walking toward the fire.

Oogo's father looked at the fish hanging over the flames. "Ughh!" Oogo's father grunted.   He grabbed the stick, pulled it from the fire, and laid it on a rock next to Oogo.

Oogo looked at the fish, then at his dad. His father shook his head in disgust. He took his spearhead knife and tried to scrape off the burned fish skin.

"Ummm?" Oogo's father stopped for a moment and smelled the fish then scratched his head. He tore a small piece off and chewed on it. "Ummm!" he smiled and handed some to everyone else.

"Ummm!" Everyone smiled, placed their fish on sticks, and hung them out over the fire too.

A loud terrifying growl echoed into the cave. A hungry Saber tooth tiger had smelled the cooking fish and had followed its scent.

Oogo's father and the other men grabbed their spears and ran toward the cave opening. They looked out into the darkness. They could hear the big tiger but they

CHRISTY DAVIS

19

could not see him. Oogo wanted to help. He quickly grabbed a wooden club from the edge of the fire and

raced to the opening. He stood next to his father and peered out into the darkness.

Oogo felt something stinging his hand. When he looked to see what it was, he noticed the club was on fire and tiny glowing red specks were landing on him. Oogo held the club straight out, away from his body, so the specks wouldn't hurt him anymore. That's when he saw the Saber tooth tiger nearly on top of him. Oogo's heart almost jumped out of his chest and he froze in fear.

Instead of running Oogo closed his eyes and the huge tiger's face hit the end of the club. The flame burned his whiskers and scorched his fur. The Saber tooth jumped back in fear. He turned and ran down the mountain as fast as he could go.

Oogo could hear his father and the other men laughing and he opened his eyes. He asked where the tiger had gone, and his father pointed down the mountain. Oogo handed the club to his father. He'd learned a long time ago not to play with fire. He only liked fire inside the cave where his father and the other men

Oogo's father and mother gave him a big hug. They were very proud of their son. Not only did they learn how to cook fish (even Oogo liked the taste of cooked fish) they also learned how to use fire as a weapon.

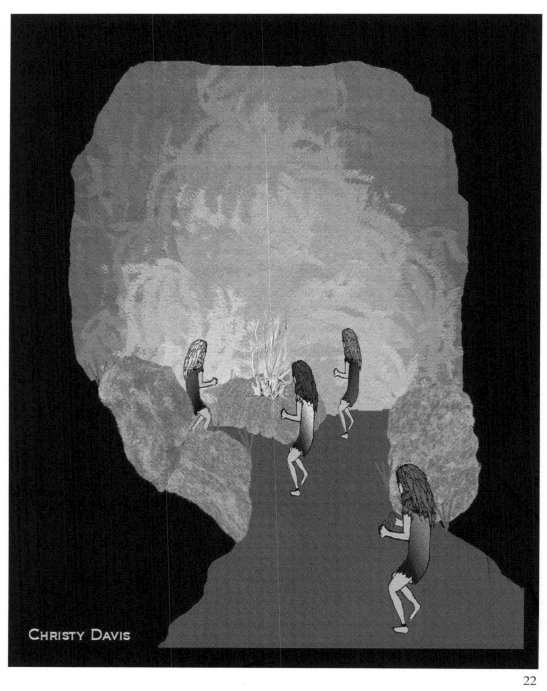

CHRISTY DAVIS

STORY 3

Oogo was a small cave boy. He was seven summers old. He had long tangled dark brown hair and hazel green eyes. He wore a tiger skin and walked barefoot everywhere he went.

Oogo lived with his father and mother in a large cave up on the side of a big mountain. Four other people lived in the cave with them. Oogo was the only child.   Everyone helped find food and fight the big animals that came to eat them. They never let Oogo help, everyone thought that Oogo was too young.

One sunny afternoon, Oogo sat on the ledge outside his cave and waited for his father. Oogo's father and the other two men had left early that morning to go hunting. They had taken their spears and knives with them.

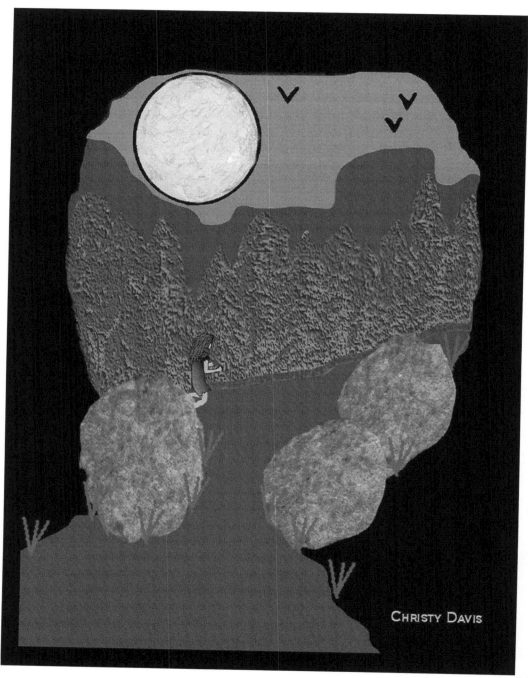

CHRISTY DAVIS

Oogo's mother and the other two women were inside the cave painting pictures on the walls. They'd sent him outside to play. He was in the way.

Oogo didn't care. Instead of being upset he sat on the ledge making spearheads for his father, and dreamed of the day he could go hunting with the men. He watched for his father as he worked.

Oogo had just chipped out three good spearheads. As he set the last one down in the dirt next to him, he looked up and saw his father and the other men walking over a far hill.

Oogo ran inside the cave to tell his mother and the other women. Everyone hurried out to the ledge and cheered as the hunting party drew closer.

Oogo suddenly felt the earth shake underneath his feet. He slipped and tumbled off the ledge. He rolled down the mountain a few feet before grabbing onto some brush to stop himself. That's when he heard his mother scream, and he looked up at the cave.

A huge dinosaur with a great big head, a mouth stuffed full of sharp jagged teeth, and a long tail. It was after the women, and they ran back into the cave to hide.

The dinosaur was so big that every time it took a step the earth would shake. Oogo watched as beast tried to stick his head into the cave, but it was way too big to fit. Then it tried to stick its arm into the cave, but it was way too short to reach the women. The dinosaur roared in anger and beat at the cave opening with its tail.

Oogo knew his mother needed help fast, but he was the only one there. He had to go get his father and the other men, and he had to hurry!

He quickly climbed down the mountain to a path, and ran as fast as he could. He heard the dinosaur making horrible sounds behind him as he ran, and when he looked back over his shoulder he saw that the dinosaur was no longer up at the cave. It was chasing him!

Oogo's heart beat wildly. He knew he was too little to out run the beast. He needed a place to hide. But where?

CHRISTY DAVIS

Oogo followed different paths. He ran back and forth, here and there trying to stay out of its reach. He ran past a stream, through the bushes and up over a hill, but the dinosaur was still chasing him.

Oogo darted underneath some trees. He jumped over a log and ran down through a ditch, then he followed a small narrow path between two large pits of black-smelly-sticky stuff.   And when he reached the other side, he accidently twisted his ankle. Dropping to the ground, he turned back around to see where the dinosaur was.

The huge beast was racing toward the narrow path, and heading straight for him! Oogo crawled behind a big rock, his heart beating so hard he thought it would burst. He peeked

CHRISTY DAVIS

around one side of the giant boulder and watched as the dinosaur came closer and closer and closer.

Oogo couldn't close his eyes. He couldn't turn away, and there was no way out!

The dinosaur charged across the path wildly, stumbling into the black-smelly-sticky stuff as it went. With each step it sank deeper and deeper until it sank so deep the whole entire dinosaur was gone.

It disappeared, right in front of Oogo's eyes!

Oogo's father and the other men ran up the path with their spears and knives in their hands, ready for combat. They found Oogo hiding behind a large rock, but no matter how hard they tried, they could not find the dinosaur.

"Ughh?" Oogo's father grunted at him. He wanted to know what happened to the dinosaur.

Oogo shrugged and pointed to the black-smelly-sticky stuff where the dinosaur had been a few moments earlier. Only a large bubble remained atop the tar pit now.

"Ughhh?" Oogo's father grunted and pointed at the pit.

Oogo nodded.

Oogo's father scratched his head and smiled. The men sat and waited for the dinosaur to come back. But it never did.

Oogo's father gave him a big hug. He picked Oogo up on his shoulders, and carried him back up the mountain to the cave, and to his mother. He was very proud of his son. Now they knew one more way to protect themselves from the dinosaurs.

THE END

***

ABOUT THE AUTHOR

Hi, my name is Christy Davis. My children's books are fiction and full of mystery, adventure, fun and excitement. They're thrilling, chilling, scary, spooky and funny. They're about treasure hunts, pirates, caves, mountain men, monsters, scary monsters, possessed houses, good ghosts, bad ghosts, girls, boys, dogs, cats, rats, bats, agents, secret agents, spies, kid reporters, good guys, bad guys, graveyards, cave boys, dinosaurs, saber-tooth tigers, notes in bottles, haunted mansions, secret passageways, stormy nights and action packed days. The kids find themselves jumping, running, being chased, running, hiding, falling, (a lot of screaming and running,) setting booby traps, spying on people, inventing things, reporting and writing stories, investigating, problem solving, and solving mysteries. They learn how to depend on each other. They attend funerals and weddings, blow up science labs, sword fight with pirates, build rafts, swim, dive off yard arms, capture ghosts, solve old mysteries, create fire and weapons, fish, play chess and still manage to stay alive so I can bring them all back again for part II!

They are fun filled, action packed, mystery adventures about Ordinary Kids on Extraordinary Adventures.   My books are available online in ebook, paperback, and audiobook forms. They are available at all major online book stores. You will love them.

They include:

*The Mountain of Stone

*Newshounds

*Newshounds 2

*Edgar

*Edgar 2

*Scary Story

*Scary Story 2

*Oogo the Cave Boy

*Online and Offline Advertising and Book Promotion

*Writing Prompts for Kids

*Writing Prompts

*Writing Prompts 2

*Blog Topics, Subjects, Ideas and Writing Prompts

*Scavenger Hunts for Kids

*Treasure Hunts for Kids

*Halloween Jokes and Riddles for Kids

*Christmas Jokes and Riddles for Kids

*Scary Funny Jokes and Riddles for Kids

*Midnight Chillers 1

*Midnight Chillers 2

*And there are more books on the way.

*Plus I have an entire line of softcover journals, diaries, and notebooks available. Please visit my website to find links to my journals, my books, and all of my free print and play games, word searches, mazes, crossword puzzles and more.

* * *

So whenever you are ready
Follow me. Let me take you on an adventure!
Ordinary kids on extraordinary adventures!
Christy Davis
ChristyDavisBooks.com

Printed in Great Britain
by Amazon.co.uk, Ltd.,
Marston Gate.